Good Night, Pippin

Story and Pictures by
Joan Elizabeth Goodman

A GOLDEN BOOK · NEW YORK

Western Publishing Company, Inc., Racine, Wisconsin 53404

For my parents
and
Richard, with love.

"Good night, Pippin," said Mama.
"I'm not sleepy," said Pippin. "Please tell me a story."
"All right," said Mama. "I will tell you a story."

"Tell me about when I was a baby," said Pippin.
"When you were a baby," began Mama, "I wrapped you
snug in fleecy wool and rocked you to sleep every night."
"Now tell about the Pirates," said Pippin.

"One night the Pirates came and stole you away,"
said Mama.

"But you heard them take me," said Pippin.
"And I ran after you," said Mama.

"I hid in the dark, fishy hold of the Pirate ship, all the
way across the deep green seas to Smuggler's Reef."

"Then the Pirates ate me," said Pippin.

"No," said Mama. "They made a circle and began
dancing around you.

"While they danced, I disguised myself as a palm tree."

"Then you pounded the Pirates with coconuts,"
said Pippin.

"I didn't have to," said Mama. "I leapt into their circle, flapping palm fronds and bellowing,

PIRATES BEWARE!

Then the Pirates went all silly with fright. They shook in their boots. They whimpered and wailed. And they promised never to steal babies ever again, if only the palm trees would leave them alone.''

"And then we went home," said Pippin.

"Yes," said Mama. "We took the Pirate ship and sailed back over the deep green seas, all the way home."

"Now tell me about how Papa saved me from the Wizard," said Pippin.

"And will that make you sleepy?" asked Mama.

"Oh, yes," said Pippin.

"When you were still a baby," said Mama, "Papa took you out to play in the sunshine."

"Where were you?" asked Pippin.

"I was at market," said Mama, "when the evil Wizard
came by and turned you into stone.

"He put you on his magic sled and soared off around the wide world to his castle in the Purple Mountains."

"Then Papa built a plane," said Pippin.

"Yes," said Mama. "He built a plane with many wings, and he flew around the wide world to rescue you.

"He came to the Wizard's castle at twilight, and found you all alone in the garden."

"Where was the Wizard?" asked Pippin.

"The Wizard was in his kitchen, making soup," said Mama. "Papa tiptoed past him to the pantry.

"In a book there, he found a spell to bring you back to life."

"Then we flew away home," said Pippin.

"No," said Mama. "First Papa cast a spell that kept the Wizard's soup from ever getting hot.

"Then he ran to you in the garden. He spoke the good spell over you, and the stone melted away."

"And then we flew away home," said Pippin.

"Yes," said Mama. "Then you and Papa flew back around the wide world and were home before I got back from market."

"What happened to the Wizard?" asked Pippin.

"The Wizard is still waiting for his supper," said Mama.

"Isn't he terribly hungry?" asked Pippin.

"Mostly he is vexed," said Mama. "Anyway, he is too busy tending his soup ever to bother us again."

"Now tell me the Galactian story," said Pippin.
"And then will you go to sleep?" asked Mama.
"Then I will go to sleep," said Pippin.
"One day..." began Mama.
"When I was a baby," said Pippin.

"When you were a baby," said Mama, "a Galactian spaceship landed on our house."

"The Galactians had freeze beams," said Pippin.

"And ears that nearly touched their turned-up toes," said Mama.

"They froze Papa in the attic," said Pippin.

"And they froze me in the hall," said Mama.

"But they didn't freeze me," said Pippin.

"No," said Mama. "Because you were playing your tambourine.

"When the Galactians got to your room, they dropped their freeze beams, rolled up their ears, and cried orange tears."

"They were scared," said Pippin.

"And the sound of your tambourine hurt their ears," said Mama.

"They tried to pull it away from you, and you began to scream."

"I screamed really loud," said Pippin.

"Yes," said Mama. "And it drove the Galactians wild.

"They begged you to stop."
"But I wouldn't," said Pippin.
"No, you wouldn't," said Mama.

"So they scrambled back into their spaceship and
zoomed off to invade a quieter planet."

"Then you and Papa came unfrozen," said Pippin.

"And we both ran to you and held you tight," said Mama. "Then I wrapped you in fleecy wool and rocked you to sleep."

"And you kissed me good night," said Pippin.
"And I kissed you good night," said Mama.
"Good night, Mama," said Pippin.
"Good night, Pippin," said Mama.